For Umma and Ahbuji,
my mom and dad

BLOOMSBURY CHILDREN'S BOOKS
Bloomsbury Publishing Inc., part of Bloomsbury Publishing Plc
1385 Broadway, New York, NY 10018

BLOOMSBURY, BLOOMSBURY CHILDREN'S BOOKS, and the Diana logo
are trademarks of Bloomsbury Publishing Plc

First published in the United States of America in September 2022
by Bloomsbury Children's Books

Text and illustrations copyright © 2022 by Salina Yoon

Bloomsbury books may be purchased for business or promotional use.
For information on bulk purchases please contact Macmillan Corporate and
Premium Sales Department at specialmarkets@macmillan.com

Library of Congress Cataloging-in-Publication Data
available upon request
ISBN 978-1-68119-344-1 (hardcover) • ISBN 978-1-68119-977-1 (e-book)
• ISBN 978-1-68119-978-8 (e-PDF)

Art created digitally using Adobe Photoshop
Typeset in Maiandra
Book design by Jeanette Levy and Nicole Gastonguay
Printed in China by Leo Paper Products, Heshan, Guangdong
2 4 6 8 10 9 7 5 3 1

To find out more about our authors and books
visit www.bloomsbury.com and sign up for our newsletters.

Penguin and Penelope

Salina Yoon

BLOOMSBURY
CHILDREN'S BOOKS

NEW YORK LONDON OXFORD NEW DELHI SYDNEY

One day, Penguin came
across a little elephant.

Her name was Penelope.

Penguin helped her get unstuck.

He gave her food,

water,

and a bath.

"Let's get you home," said Penguin.
Penguin followed the tracks that
the herd left behind.

The tracks led them to a ravine
that was too wide to cross.
"Oh dear," said Penguin.
"We'd better find another way."

Each day, they walked for miles to find another way home for Penelope . . .

. . . but there was no path around the ravine.

"Let's rest," said Penguin.

Over time, their friendship grew and grew, and so did Penelope.

Wherever Penguin went,
Penelope followed.

As they were lying on the beach, birds flew overhead.

"I wish we could fly like those birds!" said Penelope.

Penguin had an idea.

"Come with me!" said Penguin.
Penelope was unsure about the water.
It looked cold and deep.

Penelope stopped when the water reached her knees, but Penguin asked her to trust him.

And she did.

It was like magic.

They swam clear across to the other side.
When they stepped out of the water, they
found something on the ground.

"Elephant tracks!" shouted Penguin.

Penguin and Penelope followed them.

The tracks went past the trees,

and through tall grass.

Finally, they found the herd.
Penelope was home.

"Goodbye, Penguin," said Penelope. "I'll never forget you, because elephants never forget!"

"Goodbye, Penelope," said Penguin. "I'll never forget you either, because you're unforgettable."

Penelope's family welcomed her back
with trumpeting trunks.
"How we've missed you!" they cried.

But Penelope had a hole in her heart
that was the size of a penguin.

So one day, Penelope followed
the tracks back to the water . . .

. . . and *flew*
like the birds . . .

. . . with Penguin again.

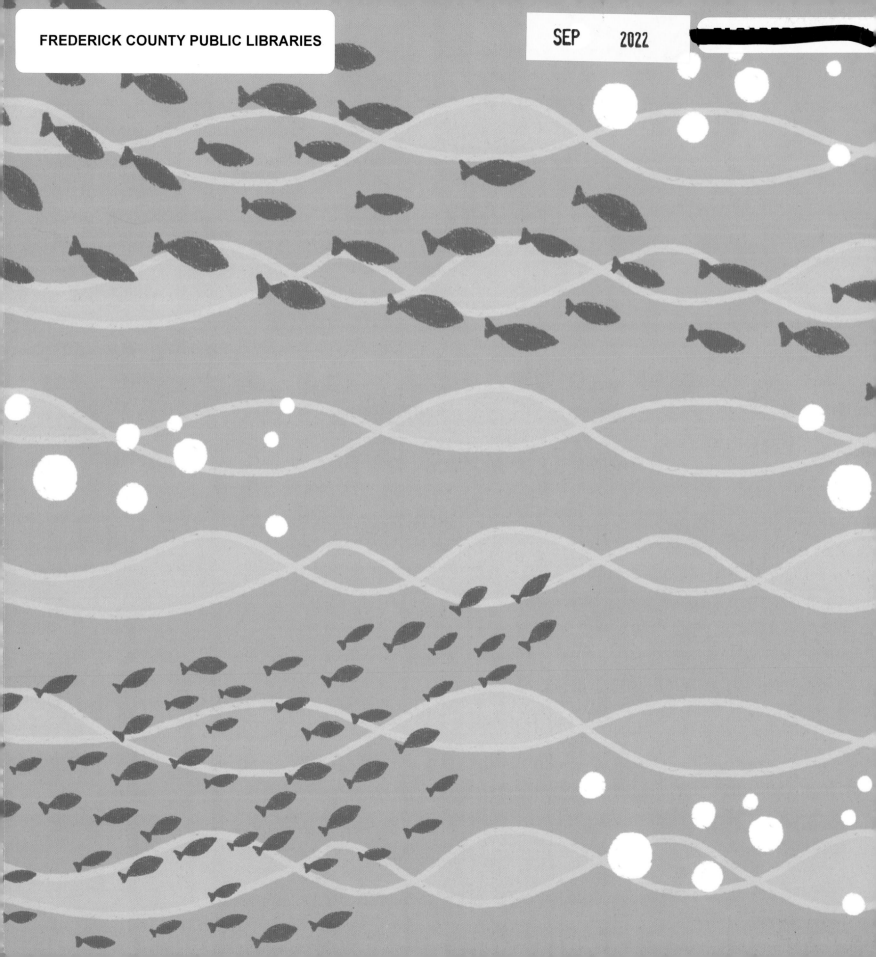